SUPER CHICKEN NUGGET BOY

and the Furious Fry

by **JOSH LEWIS**

illustrated by **DOUGLAS HOLGATE**

Disney • HYPERION BOOKS

NEW YORK

For my mom,
who taught me how to stand up to bullies

And for my dad,
who taught me when to run from them

Text copyright © 2010 by Josh Lewis
Illustrations copyright © 2010 by Douglas Holgate

First Edition
1 3 5 7 9 10 8 6 4 2
V567-9638-5-10046

This book is set in 13 point Excelsior.

Printed in the United States of America
Library of Congress Cataloging-in-Publication Data on file
ISBN 978-1-4231-1491-8 (hardcover)
ISBN 978-1-4231-1492-5 (paperback)
Reinforced binding

Visit www.hyperionbooksforchildren.com

1

THE CALM BEFORE THE STORM

It was 10:43 in the morning in Gordonville. At Bert Lahr Elementary School, everyone was doing all the things they did every school day.

Mr. Hirdleman, a second grade teacher, was getting mad at students who were making fake beards out of tape instead of learning long division. "This is math class!" he yelled. "Not wearing-fake-beards-made-out-of-tape class!"

Mrs. Sneap, a first grade teacher, was talking to her students about her cat, Mr. Pumblechook.

"I think Mr. Pumblechook is mad at me," she said. "He hasn't spoken to me in four days."

Mrs. Sneap was a little crazy.

In Mr. Zwerkle's music class, three third grade boys and one third grade girl were having a secret burping contest while the rest of the class sang a song about Switzerland.

Meanwhile, out on the playground, where it was fourth grade recess, Dirk Hamstone was about to challenge the new kid, Fernando Goldberg, to a fight.

Most people call him Fern.

2
THE CHALLENGE

Why did Dirk Hamstone want to beat Fern up? Good question. The answer: nobody knew. Nobody knew why Dirk did any of the mean things he did. He just always did them.

Fern was spending recess hanging out with his new friends, Lester McGregor and Roy Clapmist.

That day, Fern had been having a contest with Lester to see who could raise his eyebrows the highest. Roy was the judge.

Lester was winning. "Don't mess with the brow master!" he said.

"You have an unfair advantage," Fern complained. "Your eyes are lower on your face."

"He's got a point," said Roy.

"No way," said Lester. "I just have unbelievably powerful eyebrow muscles."

It was true. Lester did have unbelievably powerful eyebrow muscles. If there were an eyebrow-lifting competition in the Olympics, he would have won the gold every time.

Unfortunately, Fern and Lester had to cut their eyebrow-raising battle short when Dirk Hamstone and

HI. I'M ROY CLAPMIST.

his annoying sidekick, Donald "Snort" Boygle, walked up to them.

The only person at Bert Lahr Elementary School who was as annoying as Dirk Hamstone was Snort Boygle. He was just as mean as Dirk, and he snorted when he laughed.

"Yo!" said Dirk to Fern. "You and me, after school, at the edge of the woods, down by the creek."

That was Dirk's favorite place to beat people up—the edge of the woods, down by the creek.

Because he was the new kid at Bert Lahr Elementary School, Fern had no idea what it meant to be invited by Dirk Hamstone to the edge of the woods, down by the creek. So he just smiled at Dirk and said, "Cool. What are we going to do there?"

"What are we going to do there?" Dirk said with a laugh.

"What are you going to do there?" Snort yelled.

"We're going to fight," said Dirk. "That's what we're going to do there."

"Oh . . ." said Fern, as the smile left his

face. He turned to Lester. "I don't get it."

Snort shook his head. "Yeah, right, you don't get it. I don't believe that for a second!"

But Fern really didn't get it.

You see, the thing is, nobody questioned Dirk Hamstone. *Nobody*. It just wasn't done. When Dirk wanted something, he got it. Unfortunately for Fern, he was about to learn how Dirk always got what he wanted.

"So, what's it going to be, worm?" asked Dirk.

Snort snorted.

"Shut it, Snort Boy!" screamed Dirk; then he turned back to Fern. "So? Are you going to fight me or not?"

"I'd kind of rather not," said Fern.

"Rather not?" Snort said. *"Snort! Snort!"*

"I told you to shut it, Snort Vader!"

"Sorry, Dirk. *Snort!* Oops. Sorry for that one, too. *Snort!* And that one. Sometimes I just can't help it. *Snort! Snort!* Okay, I'm done . . . *Snort!*"

Snort finally shut his snort-hole.

That was when Dirk made his move. His eyes went all creepy and squinty, and he got right up in Fern's face.

"Okay, fine, don't fight me," he said. "Then I'll just be forced to tell my dad!"

"Oh," said Fern. "Who's your dad?"

"You've got to be kidding me! You've got to be kidding me!" said Snort.

"I'm not kidding," said Fern. "I've only been going to this school for a week and a half. I don't know everybody."

"Oh, well," said Dirk, "he's nobody too important. Just Principal Hamstone! Principal of the entire school!"

"I see," said Fern.

"And he does whatever I tell him to," said Dirk, "including giving detentions!"

Fern felt his stomach suddenly churning. Even though he was new at Bert Lahr Elementary, he'd already heard all about detention. Detention meant staying after school for two whole hours in a classroom ruled by the gym teacher, Mr. Pummel.

"And not just one detention," said Dirk, "but

weeks or months or even years of detention!"

That, right there, was how Dirk always got what he wanted.

Fern remembered a story Lester had told him about a time that he'd had detention. . . .

Dirk wasn't kidding about the detentions, either.

Just two days earlier, in the alley behind Bogie's Burger Barn, Dirk had told Farnsworth Yorb to jump into the grungy, above-the-ground-pool-type thingy with the green gooey liquid inside.

There's one thing you need to understand: no one in their right mind would ever jump into the grungy, above-the-ground-pool-type thingy with the green gooey liquid inside.

Why? Because . . .

A) It's grungy.

B) It's got green gooey liquid inside. And not just any ordinary green gooey liquid, either; green gooey liquid that bubbles and hisses and oozes over the sides of the above-the-ground-pool-type thingy.

Farnsworth was no dummy. He said, "No!"

HELLO, I'M PRINCIPAL MURKWOOD HAMSTONE. BUT YOU CAN JUST CALL ME MURKEY.

That was when Dirk went home and told his dad.

"You need to give Farnsworth Yorb seven and a half months of detention," he said.

"Why?" asked Principal Hamstone.

"Because," said Dirk, "he wouldn't jump into the grungy, above-the-ground-pool-type thingy with the green gooey liquid inside."

"What?" said Principal Hamstone. "No.

I can't give a boy seven and a half months of detention because he showed some common sense. Who in their right mind would jump into a grungy, above-the-ground-pool-type thingy with green gooey liquid inside?"

"You're not going to help me?" asked Dirk.

"No," said Principal Hamstone.

So Dirk did what he always did when he wanted to get something from his dad: he went and told his mom.

When Dirk told his mom that his dad wouldn't give Farnsworth Yorb seven and a half months of detention for refusing to jump into the grungy, above-the-ground-pool-type thingy with the green gooey liquid inside, Dirk's mom did exactly what Dirk knew she would do: she went to talk to his dad.

When Principal Hamstone said, "But, darling, I can't give a boy seven and a half months of detention just because he won't jump into a grungy, above-the-ground-pool-type thingy with green gooey liquid inside," Mrs. Hamstone did what she always did when she wanted to get something from Principal Hamstone.

She screamed, "MURRRRKWOOOOD!" at the top of her lungs until Principal Hamstone couldn't take it anymore and gave her what she wanted.

Fern stood opposite Dirk Hamstone and thought about detention and Mr. Pummel and trying not to breathe, and he wondered, What's worse? Getting beat up for a *minute* or being stuck in detention for a *year*?

And that was how Fern ended up fighting Dirk Hamstone.

And now, please welcome Harvey Zwerkle.

The song is called "Fern Went Down to Fight Dirk Hamstone," and it's sung to the tune of "I've Been Working on the Railroad." Remember: this is a sing-along.

You have to sing!

Okay, ready? And, five, six, seven, eight!

FERN WENT DOWN TO FIGHT DIRK HAMSTONE
OVER DOWN BY THE CREEK.
FERN WENT DOWN TO FIGHT DIRK HAMSTONE
BECAUSE DIRK WAS SUCH A CREEP.
THE FIGHT ENDED JUST AFTER IT STARTED,
WHEN FERN RAN AT DIRK WITH GLEE;
DIRK STEPPED ASIDE, AND FERN KEPT GOING,
RAN INTO A TREE!
OH!
RAN INTO A TREE!
RAN INTO A TREE!
RAN INTO A TREE!
. . . A TREE!
RAN INTO A TREE!
RAN INTO A TREE!
FERN RAN INTO A TREE!

3

THAT'S NO WAY TO TREE A PERSON

Fern didn't just run into a tree, either. He fell into the creek right afterward.

That put an end to the fight—which hadn't really ever begun. Even a guy as nasty as Dirk Hamstone didn't see any point in beating up a kid who had just run into a tree and fallen into a creek and was now stumbling around, all wet and dizzy.

For days after the fight, everyone at school talked about whether Fern was better or worse off because he'd avoided getting beaten up by running into a tree.

In the end, most kids decided it was a

toss-up. That is, until Lester McGregor set them straight. "As much as it would stink to get beat up by a tree," said Lester, "at least when it's over, it's over. It's not like the tree is going to follow you home."

Dirk Hamstone was another story completely.

The day after the fight, Fern saw Dirk in action again. This time Gerard Venvent was his victim. Dirk wanted Gerard to put creamed corn in his armpits. When Gerard said no, Dirk didn't hesitate for a second.

"Principal Hamstone!" Dirk called out to his dad. "Principal Hamstone!"

Dirk always called his dad Principal Hamstone at school to make it seem like he was just another kid. Yeah, right!

Principal Hamstone was busy talking to one of the women dishing out the hot lunch. "I've got to tell you, June, you're the best pizza-burger-lunch-lady server we've ever had at this school. Keep up the great work!"

"Principal Hamstone!" Dirk called out again.

Principal Hamstone let out a deep sigh. "What is it?" he asked, walking over to Dirk.

Dirk pointed at Gerard. "He won't put creamed corn in his armpits!" he said.

"Good for him," said Principal Hamstone. "Why would he want to put creamed corn in his armpits?"

"Because I want him to put creamed corn in his armpits!" said Dirk.

"Oh . . ." said Principal Hamstone. "Well . . . uh . . . what am I supposed to do about it?"

"Give him detention!" yelled Dirk.

"I can't just give him detention for not putting creamed corn in his armpits," said Principal Hamstone. "It wouldn't be right."

"Thank you," said Gerard as he went back to eating his lunch.

Dirk got up on his tippy-toes and whispered into Principal Hamstone's ears, "Don't make me tell Mommy."

Principal Hamstone suddenly pictured his

wife standing over him that night, screaming:

MURKWOOOOD!!

Before Gerard even got a chance to bite into his peanut-butter-and-Swiss-cheese sandwich, Principal Hamstone shrugged his shoulders and sighed, "Six months of detention, Gerard."

"But . . ." said Gerard. It was no use. Principal Hamstone was already walking out of the lunchroom.

Dirk stood there, laughing. Just like his mom, he knew exactly what to say to his dad to get what he wanted.

Fern and Lester had watched the Gerard Venvent incident go down from the safety of the other side of the lunchroom.

"Phew," Fern said. "Good thing I let him fight me. That ought to at least let me off the hook for a while."

"Yeah," said Lester.

But nothing could've have been further from the truth.

4
FERN'S MISFORTUNES

Maybe it was because Dirk was mad that he hadn't gotten to beat Fern up himself. Maybe it was because he had bullied every other kid in the school and Fern was a new and exciting kid to bully. Or maybe it was just because he was bored. Whatever the reason, Dirk wouldn't leave Fern alone.

Within just a couple of days after the fight, Dirk, with Snort's help, started doing everything in his power to make Fern's life completely and utterly miserable.

That's how it went for the next two and a half weeks: Dirk getting Fern to ram his head into a wall for no reason, Snort getting Fern to glue his hand to his face, Dirk getting Fern to wash his hair with sand. It was never-ending.

But then one day, something happened. Dirk pushed it just a little too far.

5

ARNIE SIMPSON: PET SUPREME

This is Arnie Simpson, the salamander.

I CAN'T TALK. I'M A SALAMANDER.

Arnie Simpson the Salamander was Fern's class pet. He was a seriously cool pet. He was friendly, slimy, extremely rubbery, and everybody in the class thought he was totally excellent—except Janice Oglie, Winnie Kinney, and Donna Wergnort.

And even Donna Wergnort secretly liked Arnie. She only pretended not to like him because Winnie and Janice said Arnie was ugly and gross, and they were Donna's best friends, and Donna always did whatever Winnie and Janice did, whether she wanted to or not. Even Fern's teacher, Ms. Durbindin, liked Arnie Simpson, and she hadn't been sure that she would.

But no one in the class loved Arnie Simpson the Salamander more than Fern.

There were a few reasons why Fern loved Arnie Simpson the Salamander so much. For one thing, it had been Fern's idea to get a sala-mander. For another thing, he had come up

with the name Arnie Simpson the Salamander. He said that Arnie Simpson the Salamander looked a lot like the school's janitor, whose name was also Arnie Simpson.

The third and most important reason was that Fern had had a very bad experience in his past that made him more protective of Arnie Simpson the Salamander than anyone else.

When Fern was two and three-quarters years old, he'd had a goldfish named Uncle Charlie.

Fern loved Uncle Charlie more than any-thing. He loved Uncle Charlie so much that one night he decided to bring Uncle Charlie to bed with him.

**WARNING! WARNING! WARNING!
DO NOT BRING YOUR FISH
TO BED WITH YOU!
THIS IS NOT A GOOD IDEA!**

The next morning was the worst moment of Fern's life. Waking up in bed next to your dead fish is not a fun way to start your day, whether you're two and three-quarters years old or twenty and three-quarters years old or two hundred and three-quarters years old. It stinks no matter what.

6

BIRTH OF A NUGGET

Because Arnie Simpson the Salamander needed to be fed every day, and there was nobody at school to feed him on the weekends, Ms. Durbindin let each of her students have a turn taking Arnie home with them for the weekend.

Friday was Fern's turn.

By lunchtime on the preceeding Monday, Fern was already freaking out, he was so excited to take Arnie home.

"Lester, do you think Arnie Simpson will like my house? Do you think Arnie Simpson will like my room? Do you think Arnie Simpson will like my pajamas?"

"Will you stop it, already?" Lester said. "He's a salamander! Not a human!"

"Exactly. That's what worries me, Lester! Salamanders have very different needs from humans."

It was no use trying to argue. "Will you please just try to relax and let me eat my ketchup in peace?" Lester loved ketchup, by the way.

So while Lester was eating ketchup, Fern was freaking out about Arnie Simpson.

But Fern's freak-out was nothing compared to what was about to happen.

Dirk and the Snort-a-nator walked up to Fern and Lester's table.

"Yo," Dirk said to Fern, "we need to talk about the lizard."

"He's not a lizard," said Fern. "He's a salamander."

"Whatever, same thing," said Dirk.

"Yeah, same thing!" said Snort.

"No, it isn't," said Fern. "Lizards are reptiles, and salamanders are amphibians."

"I don't care what it is," said Dirk. "I'm taking it home this weekend."

Fern froze. He didn't know what to say. He'd always given Dirk everything he wanted.

"Um . . . um . . ." he said, "but you're not even in our class."

"So what?" said Dirk. "I'm taking it."

Fern thought about it. Then he looked at Dirk, square in the eye, and said, "No."

"What did you say?" asked Dirk.

"No. You can't have him," said Fern. "I've been waiting all year for my turn, and I'm taking him home!"

"You really want detention, don't you?" said Dirk.

"No," replied Fern.

"Then you better give me what I want," said Dirk.

"Yeah! *Snort!* Give him what he wants!" said Snort.

"Shut it, Snortville!" Dirk said. Then he turned back to Fern. "You're going to be sorry. My dad's the most powerful person at

this school, and he's not going to be happy that you're making me mad."

"Yeah, well . . ." said Fern, "I know powerful people, too."

"You do?" asked Lester.

"Oh, really? And who might you know?" asked Dirk.

"Well . . ." said Fern, "I'll tell you who . . . uh . . . uh . . ."

Fern had no idea what he was saying. He

didn't know anyone powerful. He looked around the lunchroom at all of the kids eating their lunches. Maybe one of their parents was powerful and could help him.

"I'm waiting," said Dirk.

Fern was desperate. He needed to come up with somebody powerful right away.

"You're such a liar," said Dirk. "You don't know anyone powerful. I'm going to go tell my dad to give you *two years of detention* right now!"

Dirk and Snort turned and started to leave when Fern blurted out, "I know Super Chicken Nugget Boy!"

Dirk turned back around. "What did you say?"

"I said I know Super Chicken Nugget Boy," said Fern.

"Who's that?" asked Dirk.

"You don't know who Super Chicken Nugget Boy is?" asked Fern. "He's only the most powerful crime fighter in the history of Gordonville."

"Huh?" said Lester. He was completely lost. He didn't have a clue as to what his friend was talking about. He looked at Fern. Fern was staring at Dirk. Lester looked at

Dirk. Dirk glared at him. He looked down at the table.

Suddenly it hit him—he knew what Fern was up to! On the table in front of Fern was his lunch. The same lunch Fern had gotten every single day for as long as Lester had known him—chicken nuggets.

"You're so full of it," said Dirk. "There's no such thing as Super Chicken Nugget Boy."

"You'd better watch what you say about him," said Fern.

"Yeah," said Lester. "You don't want to make him angry." He looked at Fern and smiled.

"Whatever," said Dirk. "I'm not scared of no nonexistent nugget." He turned to Snort. "Come on, let's go put rocks in Stu Burns's pants."

"Yeah," said Snort.

As Dirk and Snort walked out of the lunch-room, Dirk turned back to Fern.

"You haven't heard the last of me."

"Way to go!" Lester said to Fern. "That was *so* sweet!"

"Thanks, Lester," said Fern.

"I'm just confused about one thing," said Lester.

"What?" Fern asked.

"Well," said Lester, "isn't Dirk just going to get madder when he finds out that Super Chicken Nugget Boy isn't real?"

"Maybe," said Fern. "But then again, maybe not."

"What do you mean?" Lester asked.

Fern got a sneaky look on his face and said, "When you think about it, there's no reason he needs to find out that Super Chicken Nugget Boy's not real."

"Huh?" said Lester. He noticed a mischie-
vous smile on his friend's face.

"I've got an idea," said Fern. "Come on!"

That was when he went to work.

7

THE NINJA NUGGET BATTLE

Fern spent the rest of the week devising the ultimate master plan to convince Dirk Hamstone that Super Chicken Nugget Boy was real.

The plan was very elaborate. It had to be if Fern stood any chance of fooling Dirk. It involved costumes and props and perfectly synchronized timing. It also required the aid of many of Fern's and Lester's classmates. Getting them to help was the easy part, though. All Fern had to do was tell them that he was heading up a major operation to take

down Dirk Hamstone once and for all, and the students couldn't sign up fast enough.

At the end of the day on Friday, everyone sprang into action.

The first thing Fern needed was to get Arnie Simpson the Salamander out of the school without Dirk's noticing. That was easy. He put Arnie in his pocket. When Fern passed Dirk and Snort in the hall, Dirk thought he had finally come to his senses and left Arnie Simpson for him to take home.

By the time Dirk got to Ms. Durbindin's classroom and discovered that Arnie Simpson

wasn't there, it was too late. Fern was gone. At least, that was what Dirk thought.

Ms. Durbindin was the only one left in the class. "Hey there, boys," Ms. Durbindin said to Dirk and Snort. "Can I help you with something?"

"That's okay," said Dirk.

"Are you sure?" asked Ms. Durbindin. "We have a terrific display on the Splendor of Spoons, with pretty much every kind of spoon you can imagine. Janice Oglie even got her cousin in Sweden to send her a ladle called a *skopa*. Did you know that in China they consume three hundred and twenty billion bowls of soup each year? That's a lot of spoons. Would you like to see some of ours?"

"Sure!" said Snort, walking toward the display. "That sounds awesome."

"No!" said Dirk, grabbing Snort. "We've got things to take care of."

And he pulled Snort out of the room.

Ms. Durbindin didn't realize it, but by talking to Dirk and Snort for just that minute, she was buying time for Fern to prepare phase two of his operation.

See, Fern wasn't done. He still had to show Dirk that getting his dad to give Fern detention was a very, very bad idea. Messing with Fern meant messing with Super Chicken Nugget Boy, and nobody would want that kind of trouble.

Dirk and Snort headed for Principal Hamstone's office. "Come on," said Dirk to Snort. "I'm going to get him detention for the rest of his life!"

Fern knew that Dirk would go straight to Principal Hamstone's office. He just needed to get Dirk's attention before he got there. That was where Lester came in. Fern had stationed Lester right on the edge of the playground. And while Lester stood lookout, Fern ran and hid around the corner and got into his Super Chicken Nugget Boy outfit.

Meanwhile, at the exact moment that Lester saw Dirk and Snort passing by the giant windows of the first grade hall, he pretended to be walking through the playground when, all of a sudden, he got jumped by sixteen ninjas!

Obviously they weren't real ninjas, just kids in ninja disguises who wanted to see Dirk go down just as much as Fern did. Many other kids had wanted to help, but they were all stuck in detention.

Lester screamed, "Help! Help! I'm being attacked by sixteen ninjas! Please! Help! Somebody! I'm no match for sixteen ninjas!"

Fern's plan was working perfectly. Dirk and Snort had stopped in front of the windows to watch what was going on.

"Whoa!" exclaimed Snort. "He's being attacked by sixteen ninjas!"

NO! DON'T HURT ME, YOU BRUTAL NINJAS! I'M ALLERGIC TO PAIN!

I DIDN'T KNOW GORDONVILLE EVEN HAD NINJAS!

That didn't faze Dirk, though. He stayed completely calm. "Don't worry about it," he said. "My dad will take care of it. They're violating playground policy."

That's when Fern appeared, as Super Chicken Nugget Boy.

The ninjas screamed, "Aaaghhhhhh!!!" and ran at Fern.

Thump! Crash!

Ninjas were flying everywhere!

Fern was kicking so much ninja butt he started to get carried away.

"Hiee-yah! Take that, you ninja nitwit!" he said to Roy Clapmist as he ninja-chopped him with all his might.

"Ouch!" Roy whispered through his ninja disguise. "That hurt! I thought this was pretend."

"Oh, yeah. Sorry," Fern whispered back.

A second later, Vinnie Curtis and two other ninjas jumped on Fern from behind.

Splat!

They forgot it was pretend, too.

Fern was surrounded by all sixteen ninjas.

"Foolish ninjas!" he cried out. "Don't you

realize I'm the Supreme Super Chicken Nugget Warrior of the World?"

Dirk and Snort looked on in amazement as Super Chicken Nugget Boy demolished the ninjas.

"That's one tough nugget!" said Snort.

"He's not *that* tough," said Dirk.

"But look at him knocking out all those ninjas," said Snort.

"It's not his job to knock out ninjas!" screamed Dirk. "It's my dad's job! He's the principal of this school! He's in charge!"

"He sure is," said Snort.

Dirk had an idea. "You know what? I'm going to tell that breaded bozo!"

"You are?" asked Snort.

"Yup!" said Dirk. "I'm going to tell all of them that they'd better shape up or my dad will come out here and give them all *detention*! Come on, let's go."

"Um, okay," said Snort. "Okay!"

Dirk and Snort headed out of the school toward the playground.

8
CHICKEN CHASE

The last thing anyone expected to see during the Super Chicken Nugget Boy–ninja battle was Dirk Hamstone and Snort walking out of

the school and heading right for them. That wasn't part of the plan.

"Um, Fern . . ." said Lester, trying to get Fern's attention.

"Not now, Lester," said Fern. "If I let up now, Dirk and Snort will figure out that it's all a trick."

"That's exactly what I need to talk to you about," said Lester. "They're about to figure that out anyway."

"What do you mean?" he asked.

"Look!" Lester pointed toward Dirk and Snort, who were getting closer by the second.

"Uh-oh!" said Fern.

"What are we going to do?" Lester asked.

"Let me think for a second. . . ." said Fern. "Hmmm . . . I got it! Run!!!"

Suddenly there were ninjas running in every direction. Left! Right! Away from the

school. Around the school. Ninjas bumping into each other. Ninjas jumping over each other. It was complete mayhem!

Fern and Lester ran off, but Dirk and Snort chased after them.

Dirk called out, "Come back here, Nugget Boy! I want to talk to you!"

"Yeah," said Snort. "We want to talk to you!"

"Just ignore them and keep running, Lester!" said Fern.

"Don't worry," Lester said. "I don't want

to get my face smashed into a bazillion pieces any more than you do."

Fern and Lester could hear the Snort-o-meter behind them the entire time. When the snorts grew quieter, they knew Snort and Dirk were farther away. When the snorts were louder, they knew they were closer.

Fern and Lester turned a corner.

Dirk and Snort turned the corner too.

Fern and Lester took a shortcut through a backyard.

Dirk and Snort took the same shortcut through the same backyard.

"Halt!" Dirk called out. "In the name of the son of Principal Hamstone, I order you to stop where you are!"

"Yeah!" added Snort. "And in the name of the friend of the son of Principal Hamstone, I also order you to stop!"

But Fern and Lester didn't stop. They kept running.

They ran into the parking lot of Bogie's Burger Barn.

"Quick! Follow me," said Fern as he ducked into the alley.

Lester followed right behind him.

A second later, Dirk and Snort went running past Bogie's Burger Barn and up the street. They didn't see Fern and Lester.

Fern and Lester listened to the *Snort!-Snort!-Snort!*-ing fade off into the distance.

"Phew, that was a close one," said Lester.

"You can say that again," said Fern.

"Phew, that was a close one," said Lester.

Fern shook his head and gave his friend a dirty look.

They were behind Bogie's Burger Barn for about fifteen seconds when an unbelievably disgustingly gross smell began to drift up their noses.

"Pee-yew! What is that?" asked Fern. "It stinks even worse than Richie Gallon's tree fort."

RICHIE GALLON

"It's the grungy, above-the-ground-pool-type thingy," said Lester, pointing to the very back of the alley. "Haven't you ever been back here?"

"Why would I ever come back here?" asked Fern.

"To see the grungy, above-the-ground-pool-type thingy," said Lester.

"Blech! No, thank you," said Fern as he watched the green gooey liquid ooze down the side of the pool.

9
THE BURGER BARN BOOGIE

Fern and Lester waited behind Bogie's Burger Barn for a couple of minutes, until they were sure it was safe. Finally Fern said, "Come on, Lester. Let's get out of here."

"Yeah," added Lester, "before our noses are exposed to any long-lasting permanent stinkage."

They turned to go, but before they could even take a step they heard a *Snort!-Snort!-Snort!*-ing heading in their direction.

"Uh-oh," Lester whispered.

"Uh-oh!" Fern screamed, bolting upright.

"Shhh!" said Lester. "They'll hear you."

Fern screamed again. "Yikes!" He started quaking and shaking as if he'd just been stung by a school of angry electric eels.

"Are you nuts?" Lester whispered to Fern. "What's wrong with you?"

"I don't know," said Fern. He twisted and squirmed in every possible direction. "Yow! Whoa! Ha! Ya-ya-ya!"

Meanwhile, Dirk and Snort were getting closer.

"Snort! Snort! Snort!"

Fern wiggled and wriggled. "Eeh! Ooh! Yo! My! Mee! Mo! Mumamuma!"

The snorting grew louder.

"Snort! Snort! Snort!"

What with Snort's snorting and Fern's quaking, shaking, and grunting, they sounded like some sort of demented all-star-barnyard-animal chorus.

Lester grabbed Fern and shook him. "What's your problem?" he yelled. "Have you completely lost your marbles?"

Fern shook back and forth, twisting his body into dozens of crazy positions.

"Yeow! Eeep! Snirk! Bugabugabug!"

Then they heard a thump.

They looked down at the ground. It was Arnie Simpson! He had jumped out from the bottom of Fern's Super Chicken Nugget Boy outfit.

"Of course!" said Fern. "I completely forgot. Arnie Simpson's been in my pocket ever since the end of school."

"Well, you better get him back in there," said Lester. "We've got bigger problems to worry about now."

Fern bent down to pick up Arnie, but just as he was about to grab him, the salamander ran off.

"Great!" said Fern as he chased after him.

Meanwhile, the snorting was getting closer; it was coming from just down the block.

"Snort! Snort! Snort!"

Fern tried to grab Arnie again, and again he missed.

Lester called out to Fern. "Come on! Get him! This isn't funny!"

"I'm trying," said Fern, "but he's so slippery."

Dirk and Snort ran into the Bogie's Burger Barn parking lot just as Arnie Simpson the Salamander climbed up the side of the grungy, above-the-ground-pool-type thingy. He rested at the top, along its narrow rim.

"Snort! Snort! Snort!"

Fern pulled himself up the side of the grungy, above-the-ground-pool-type thingy and crawled on his hands and knees along the narrow rim toward Arnie Simpson.

"Quick!" Lester called out.

Fern crept up on Arnie Simpson.

"Snort! Snort!"

Fern reached his hand out to Arnie. Arnie jumped into it.

"Snort! Snort! Snort!"

Fern lost his balance.

Splash!

Fern and Arnie landed right in the green gooey liquid in the grungy, above-the-ground-pool-type thingy.

10
I LOVE GOO. GOO LOVES ME.

"Well, well, well, what have we here?" asked Dirk as he and Snort appeared in the alley.

Lester slowly turned to face them.

"What do you mean?" said Snort. "That's Lester. He goes to our school."

"I know that, you snortron!" said Dirk. "It's just an expression."

"Oh," said Snort. "Yeah, I knew that." Snort hadn't known that.

Dirk glared at Lester. "We don't want to have to hurt you, Fester! We just want to know where your little chicken-boy friend is."

"Yeah!" Snort said. "Chicken-boy friend."

"You really want the truth?" Lester asked.

"Of course I want the truth," said Dirk.

"All right," said Lester. "If you really want the truth, he's inside that grungy, above-the-ground-pool-type thingy."

"Ha-ha-ha!" said Dirk. "That's not funny."

"What?" said Lester. "You said you wanted the truth."

"I'm not playing around anymore," said Dirk. "Now, where is he?"

"I already told you," said Lester.

Dirk shook his head. "You leave me no choice. If you're not going to tell us where Super Chicken Nugget Boy is, we're going to have to beat it out of you. Get him!"

"Yeah," said Snort. "Get him!"

Dirk looked at Snort. "I'm talking to you, you snort plow! *You* get him!"

"Oh," said Snort. "I get it! *I* get him. Got it."

Snort walked toward Lester, but Lester didn't even care. He was more worried about Fern. He'd been under that goo for at least a minute. Probably more.

Snort grabbed Lester from behind.

"I'm giving you one more chance, Fester," said Dirk. "Where's the nugget?"

"Why are you so obsessed with chicken nuggets?" asked Lester. "Doesn't your mommy feed you?"

"That does it!" said Dirk. "You asked for it." Dirk made a fist.

Then, just as Lester was sure he was toast, it happened.

Crash!

Suddenly, bursting out of the gooey liquid, came an enormous Super Chicken Nugget Boy! A Super Chicken Nugget Boy who was twice as big as Fern and had genuine deep-fried breading! The *real* Super Chicken Nugget Boy!

Super Chicken Nugget Boy landed on the ground in front of Lester, Dirk, and Snort.

Bam!

"Looking for me?" he asked.

"Wha—wha—wha . . ." said Snort.

"Yes, we are," said Dirk.

"What can I do for you?" asked Super Chicken Nugget Boy.

"You can watch us kick your butt!" said Dirk. "Get him, Snort!"

"But he's Super Chicken Nugget Boy!" said Snort.

"I don't care if he's Massive Meatloaf Man!" said Dirk. "I said, get him!"

"Well . . . *snort* . . . okay. If you say so."

Snort ran at Super Chicken Nugget Boy as fast as he could.

Super Chicken Nugget Boy turned sideways and delivered an awesome nugget hip bump to Snort's chest.

Bonk!

Snort went flying across the alley.

Smash!

Dirk looked at Snort. "I should've known you'd mess it up, you snort-for-nothing. Looks like I'll have to take care of this myself, as usual."

Dirk ran at Super Chicken Nugget Boy.

Super Chicken Nugget put his foot out.

Thwap!

Super Chicken Nugget Boy flicked Dirk up with his other foot.

Dirk soared through the air.

"Aieee!"

He was headed straight toward the grungy, above-the-ground-pool-type thingy.

Super Chicken Nugget Boy reached out with one of his giant, nuggety hands and grabbed him in midair.

"Let me go, you overgrown chunk of deep-fried fowl!" screamed Dirk.

"Okay," said Super Chicken Nugget Boy. "You asked for it." Super Chicken Nugget Boy opened his hand, and Dirk hurtled back down toward the grungy, above-the-ground-pool-type thingy.

Dirk was about to splash into the green gooey liquid when Super Chicken Nugget Boy reached his hand out again.

Whoosh!

He grabbed Dirk when he was just inches above the green gooey liquid.

"Still want me to let you go?" asked Super Chicken Nugget Boy.

"No! No! No!" said Dirk. "Please don't. Please, please, please!" he begged.

"All right," said Super Chicken Nugget Boy. "But if I'm going to put you back on the ground, you have to promise to take your little friend and get the heck out of here."

"I promise, I promise!" said Dirk.

"All right," said Super Chicken Nugget Boy as he put Dirk back down on the ground. "Now, get out of here. And don't let me catch you bullying kids ever again!"

"You won't," said Dirk. "That's a promise."

He grabbed Snort, who was trembling in the corner, and they ran off.

"Snort! Snort! Snort! Snort! Snort! Snort!"

"That was awesome!" said Lester.

"Thanks," said Super Chicken Nugget Boy.

The two of them stood there in silence for a moment.

"So, do you think I'll be a nugget for the rest of my life?" Super Chicken Nugget Boy finally asked.

"No," said Lester. "You're already getting less nuggety."

"Really?" asked Super Chicken Nugget Boy.

"Yeah. I can see you starting to shrink down to your unsupersize self, and your breading is flaking off all over," said Lester.

"Hmmm," said Super Chicken Nugget Boy. "I guess that's good. I mean, it would be pretty hard to explain to my parents how I all of a sudden became Super Chicken Nugget Boy."

"Yeah," said Lester. "How *did* you all of a

sudden become Super Chicken Nugget Boy, anyway?"

"I'm not sure," said Super Chicken Nugget Boy. "But it probably had something to do with this." He pointed to a sign on the side of the pool-type thingy.

"Whoa," said Lester.

"Yeah," said Super Chicken Nugget Boy.

"I noticed it when I climbed up to get Arnie Simpson the Salamander."

Super Chicken Nugget Boy and Lester suddenly looked at each other, horrified.

"Arnie!" they both yelled.

Just then . . .

Crash!

Out of the pool flew Arnie Simpson the Salamander, fifty times his normal size!

Bam!

He landed.

Lester's jaw dropped.

"Just when I thought things couldn't get any weirder," said Super Chicken Nugget Boy.

"You can say that again," said Lester.

"Just when I thought things couldn't get any weirder," said Super Chicken Nugget Boy.

11

DIRK'S DILEMMA

That night, Dirk told his dad, Principal Hamstone, about Super Chicken Nugget Boy.

"I've got more important things to worry about," said Principal Hamstone, "than some chicken vittle super guy."

"It's Super Chicken Nugget Boy," said Dirk. "And what could possibly be more important?"

"What could possibly be more important?" said Principal Hamstone. "I'll tell you. Talking to Mrs. Jackknee about why Barley Hornrim keeps sitting in trash cans in her class. Going to visit Cooper Younger at home to see how he's doing, now that they finally got the gum out of his nose. Trying to explain to Ahmed Hazari's parents why Ahmed came home today without pants! And the list goes on."

Dirk giggled because he was the one responsible for all the things his dad was upset about. He had made Barley sit in trash cans, and he had made Cooper put his gum up his nose, and he had stolen Ahmed's pants during gym class.

"Then you're not going to help me?" asked Dirk.

"No," said Principal Hamstone.

So Dirk did what he always did. He went and told his mom. She was sitting in the next room watching her favorite TV show, *Real-Life Mean People*.

"Principal Hamstone said he won't help me," Dirk told his mom. Dirk called his dad

Principal Hamstone at home, too. It made him feel cool, even though there were no other kids around to hear him.

"Well, we'll just see about that!" said Mrs. Hamstone, walking into the next room.

"What's this I hear about your not being willing to help our son?" Mrs. Hamstone asked Principal Hamstone.

"There's nothing I can do, darling," said Principal Hamstone.

"Can't you just give this Turkey Super Nugget thing a detention?"

"It's Super Chicken Nugget Boy," said Dirk.

"Stay out of this, dear," said Mrs. Hamstone.

"No," said Principal Hamstone.

"No?" repeated Mrs. Hamstone, squishing her big, red, lipsticky lips together.

"No," said Principal Hamstone.

Mrs. Hamstone then did what she always did: screamed at the top of her lungs.

"Murrrrkwoooood!"

But this time, something different happened. Instead of caving in and giving his wife what she wanted, Principal Hamstone waited for her to run out of breath. Once she did, he looked at her calmly and said, "I can't give detention to a chicken nugget that doesn't even go to the school."

Mrs. Hamstone glared at Principal Hamstone. "I can't stand it when you make sense," she said.

She grabbed Dirk and pulled him by the hand out of the room. "Come along, sweetie. It looks like this is one problem not even detention can solve."

12

FRY DAY

It was a Friday.

Ms. Durbindin was telling her class about Earle Dickson, the man who invented the Band-Aid.

"Earle Dickson may have invented the Band-Aid," said Ms. Durbindin, "but it was his clumsy wife, Josephine, who gave him the idea. She was always cutting and scraping herself. When Earle got tired of trying to cover her wounds with big, awkward bandages, he invented the Band-Aid. Now, I'm going to pass out Band-Aids to you, and you can practice putting them on your Study Buddies."

Fern's Study Buddy was Lester, but Lester wasn't there, because Ms. Durbindin had sent him to the school basement to get thumbtacks for the class's Moss Across America display. So Fern just put Band-Aids on himself.

Suddenly, Principal Hamstone's voice came over the loudspeaker.

"Your attention, please! Your attention, please! This is Principal Hamstone. I'm here to tell you that school will close immediately and stay closed until further notice.

"*The reason,*" Principal Hamstone continued, "*is because the school is being attacked by a gigantic french fry.*"

Principal Hamstone continued. "*The chess-team bake sale will be postponed until a later date, when there isn't a Furious Fry attack. Thank you.*"

The students fell silent.

Ms. Durbindin looked at the students.

The students looked at Ms. Durbindin.

Ms. Durbindin looked at the students.

"I don't know what to do," she said. "I mean, I know a lot of things. I know how to teach spelling and math and language arts. I know how to take attendance and how to do science projects using mothballs and toothpaste. I know how oat bran is made, and I know everything about the history of mustaches. I know a lot of things! But if there's one thing I do not know about, it's how to deal with a Furious Fry attack."

She took a deep breath.

"So, I'm just going to ask you all to stay calm, and I'm going to dismiss you by rows, as I always do."

Stomp!

The Furious Fry's french-fried foot came crashing down.

"AAAGH!"

Everyone ran for their lives.

Stomp! Stomp!

The entire school rattled and quaked.

Everyone could see the Furious Fry march-
ing toward the school.

The fry was so terrifying it scared the pants
off people! Really! People's pants were flying
off their bodies left and right.

The Furious Fry stomped up to the school, crushing everything in its way.

Everyone screamed in horror.

Students and teachers ran for their lives, whether they were wearing pants or not.

13
FEARLESS FERNANDO

Fern grabbed Arnie Simpson the Salamander and bolted out of the school along with Roy Clapmist.

Roy screamed as they ran, "I'm not scared! I'm not scared! I'm not scared! I'm not scared! I'm so scared! I'm so scared! I'm so scared! I'm so scared!"

Fern and Roy were halfway up the block when Fern stopped in his tracks.

"Lester!" he called out.

"What about him?" Roy asked.

"Where is he?" asked Fern.

"I don't know," said Roy. He looked around at all the kids running away from the school. "I don't see him."

"That's because he's still in school!" said Fern. "He must be trapped in the basement!"

"Oh, well," said Roy, "it was nice knowing him."

"I have to go back and get him!" said Fern.

"I think I'm losing my hearing," said Roy. "It sounded like you just said you have to go back and get Lester."

"I did," said Fern.

Roy looked at him as if he were crazy, because he was. "Have you completely lost your mind?" yelled Roy. "Do you not see that the Furious Fry is about to crush the school?"

The Furious Fry crushed seven cars with one step.

Splat! Smoosh!

Fern looked at Roy. "If I don't help Lester against that evil vegetable, who will?"

"I don't know, but that's not our problem," said Roy. "Our only problem is not getting mashed by that potato. I can't let you go back there. It's too dangerous."

Roy stood in front of Fern to block his way.

"Step aside, Roy," said Fern.

"No!" said Roy. "I won't! I'm doing this for your own good."

Fern raised his fist, the one that wasn't holding Arnie Simpson the Salamander, and put it right up to Roy's face. "I mean it!" he said.

"So do I!" said Roy, raising his fists to block Fern.

Fern pulled a switcheroo. He stomped on Roy's toe!

Roy hopped around, and Fern was able to get past him.

"I can't believe I fell for the old switcheroo," said Roy.

"Neither can I," Fern called out as he ran past Roy and back toward the terrifying tater.

14

LESTER'S RESCUE

$\int$ tomp! Stomp! Stomp!

The Furious Fry's giant steps had Fern and Arnie bouncing up and down on the pavement as if it were a cement trampoline. But that didn't stop Fern.

"Don't worry, Arnie!" he said, looking down at the salamander as they entered the school. "We'll have Lester back in a jiffy!"

Fern ran through the halls as if he were running for his life, because he was.

He turned a corner. . . .

Bam!

The Furious Fry's foot came stomping down

in the exact spot where Fern had just been.

Fern kept running.

He turned another corner and reached the door to the basement.

"Lester!" he called out. "Are you down there?"

"Yeah," Lester called up to him.

"All right," Fern said. "Don't worry! We're going to find a way to get down to you!"

"Why don't you just use the stairs?" Lester asked.

"What?" Fern said. "Oh!"

Fern ran down the stairs and found Lester sitting eating ketchup straight from the little packets.

"What are you doing?" asked Fern.

"I'm eating!" said Lester. "Look! I found all these boxes." Lester pointed to a bunch of boxes filled with little packets. "Can you believe it? It's my dream come true!"

"Are you crazy?" yelled Fern.

"No. I'm hungry," said Lester.

"We've got to get out of here!" said Fern.

"Why?" Lester asked. "And why do you have Arnie Simpson the Salamander with you?"

"Because a furious fry is about to squash the school!" said Fern.

"Yeah, right," said Lester. "Like I'm going to fall for that one?"

Stomp! Bash!

"Didn't you just hear that?" asked Fern.

"Yeah," said Lester. "It's just Mr. Pummel's gym class."

"No, it isn't!" said Fern. "Now, come on!"

Fern grabbed Lester's arm and started pulling him toward the stairs.

"Stop it!" said Lester. "I'm still hungry!"

"We have to go!" yelled Fern. He yanked Lester along.

"No-o-o-o-o-o-o-o-o-o!" screamed Lester as he jerked away, accidentally squeezing the ketchup packets he was holding right at Fern.

Splat!

Fern cried out *"AAAGHHH!"* as he grabbed his face and doubled over.

"I'm sorry," said Lester. "I didn't mean to do that. I don't know what happened. Are you okay?"

"I'm fine!" Fern shouted. "Just leave me alone! Stay here! Eat your stupid ketchup! Get squished, for all I care!"

Fern wiped the ketchup from his face and prepared to leave.

"Whoa!" said Lester.

"What?" Fern asked.

"Your face," Lester said. It was covered with breading.

Fern touched his face. "Jeez, Louise!" he said. He looked at his arms. They were covered in breading, too! Within seconds, Fern's whole body was completely covered in breading and he was more than twice his normal size!

"You're Super Chicken Nugget Boy again!" exclaimed Lester.

"Yeah," said Fern (or Super Chicken Nugget Boy, or whatever you want to call him). "How did that happen?"

"The radioactive cooking oil must still be in your system," said Lester. "It must've reacted with the ketchup and turned you back into Super Chicken Nugget Boy!"

"Yeah," said Super Chicken Nugget Boy. "That must be it! Now, let's get out of here! We've got a furious fry to foil!"

"I still don't believe you about the Furious Fry," said Lester.

Crash!

At that moment, the Furious Fry's foot smashed into the wall just inches away from Lester.

"Now I do!" said Lester. *"Let's get out of here!"*

Super Chicken Nugget Boy, Lester, and Arnie Simpson the Salamander headed up the stairs.

"Wait one second!" said Lester. He ran back and grabbed a box of ketchup packets. "Now we can go!" he said.

15
FOOD FIGHT

$\int$uper Chicken Nugget Boy, Lester, and Arnie Simpson the Salamander ran from the basement and out of the school.

Bam!

A giant, furious foot landed in front of them.

They ran right into it!

Boink!

They all went flying backward and landed in the bushes next to the playground.

Crunch!

"Terrific!" said Lester. "Just terrific! Now what do we do?"

"How should I know?" said Super Chicken Nugget Boy.

"Because you're a superhero, remember?" said Lester.

"Oh, yeah," said Super Chicken Nugget Boy. "Um . . . uh . . . well . . . all right, fine. You stay here with Arnie!"

He handed the salamander to Lester.

"It'll be my pleasure," said Lester.

"And I'll go deal with"—Super Chicken Nugget Boy pointed at the Furious Fry and gulped—"that thing."

Super Chicken Nugget Boy bulked up his breading to the best of his ability, walked up to the Furious Fry, and stood in front of him.

"All right, you treacherous tater, I'll give you two choices. One, you can leave Gordonville immediately and never come back. Or, two, you can leave Gordonville immediately and never come back. Which is it going to be?"

The Furious Fry kicked Super Chicken Nugget Boy and sent him sailing.

Boosh!

Super Chicken Nugget Boy landed in the school Dumpster.

"That does it!" he said. "From now on, I'm ordering onion rings."

He ran at the Furious Fry.

"AAAAGHHHHH!!!!"

He smacked and hacked away at the Furious Fry. Well . . . at the parts of the Furious Fry that he could reach, that is.

"Take that, you pitiful potato!"

Bip! Bap! Slap! Smack!

The Furious Fry didn't budge.

Then . . .

Blam!

He whacked Super Chicken Nugget Boy, sending him soaring.

Squish, right on top of Lester and Arnie.

Super Chicken Nugget Boy climbed off Lester and Arnie Simpson the Salamander just as Lester started to scream, "Aaagh!"

"What is it?" asked Super Chicken Nugget Boy.

"Can't you see?" said Lester. "I'm covered in blood!"

"Don't be ridiculous," said Super Chicken Nugget Boy. "That's just your ketchup from the box."

"Oh," said Lester. "I knew that. Ha-ha-ha! Of course I knew that." He hadn't known that.

Lester wiped some ketchup from his face and put it in his mouth. "Mmm, delicious," he said.

"This is no time for ketchup," said Super Chicken Nugget Boy. "We've got a serious problem on our hands."

"How can anyone have problems when they have ketchup?" said Lester.

The Furious Fry started clomping toward the Nugget, the boy, and the salamander.

"Oh, yeah," said Lester. "I forgot about him. I guess the ketchup can wait."

"Hold on! That's it!" yelled Super Chicken Nugget Boy.

"Yeah!" Lester yelled back. "What's it?" he asked.

"Ketchup!" said Super Chicken Nugget Boy.

"Huh?" asked Lester.

"Quick!" said Super Chicken Nugget Boy. "Give me Arnie!"

"Fine," said Lester, handing Arnie off to Super Chicken Nugget Boy.

"Now give me the box of ketchup!" said Super Chicken Nugget Boy.

"Are you nuts?" Lester asked. "What do you need that for?"

The Furious Fry was closing in on them.

"No time to explain!" said Super Chicken Nugget Boy. "Just give me the box!"

"But . . . but . . . but . . ." said Lester.

"Your ketchup or your life!" said Super Chicken Nugget Boy. "Which is more important?"

Stomp!

"Well?" Super Chicken Nugget Boy asked Lester.

"I'm thinking. . . ." Lester said.

The Furious Fry was just a step away from them.

"Here!" Lester gave the box to Super Chicken Nugget Boy.

"Thanks!" said Super Chicken Nugget Boy. "Now it's time to teach this fried freak the true meaning of Happy Meal."

Super Chicken Nugget Boy took the box along with Arnie and started running in the opposite direction from Lester and the Furious Fry.

"Where are you going?" screamed Lester.

"Just trust me!" Super Chicken Nugget Boy yelled back. "Try to relax!"

The Furious Fry lifted one of his giant french-fried feet.

"Try to relax! That's a good one!" shouted Lester. "I got a massive french-fried foot

about to squash me to smithereens, and you want me to relax!"

Super Chicken Nugget Boy ran onto a seesaw on the playground, picked up a huge rock, and threw it on the other end of the teeter-totter.

Bam!

"Whoa! Nelly!" he screamed as the seesaw flipped up, sending him and Arnie flying into the air.

Whoosh!

"What in the name of sailing Super Nuggets . . ." Lester said, looking up in awe.

"This is the only way to travel!" said Super Chicken Nugget Boy.

Meanwhile, the Furious Fry's foot was dangling in the air above Lester like a giant fried blimp.

Super Chicken Nugget Boy reached into Lester's ketchup-packet box, pulled out a packet of ketchup, and squeezed it on Arnie.

Splat!

In an instant, just like Super Chicken Nugget Boy, Arnie Simpson the Salamander was transformed. He changed from his little salamander self to Arnie the Awesome Amphibian, now fifty times his normal size.

"Welcome back, my slimy, courageous companion!" said Super Chicken Nugget Boy.

Meanwhile, the Furious Fry's foot cut through the air as it started to make its way back down, toward the top of Lester's head.

Lester screamed, "I don't want to be a Lester pancake! I don't taste good, and I'm allergic to syrup!"

Super Chicken Nugget Boy jumped onto Arnie the Awesome Amphibian's back, and they glided through the air together. "All right, Arnie," he said. "Let's thrash this furious failure Bert Lahr Elementary School style!"

The Furious Fry's foot was just about to squash Lester when Super Chicken Nugget Boy and Arnie the Awesome Amphibian passed right in front of its face.

Super Chicken Nugget Boy unleashed a colossal ketchup blast.

It lashed the fry right in the eyeball.

The Furious Fry lost its balance and cried out, *"Uuurrrgh!"*

Stomp!

It missed squashing Lester to bits by an inch.

"Way to go, Arnie!" said Super Chicken Nugget Boy. "I won't say he didn't know what hit him, because he's a fry, and it's ketchup. He knows exactly what hit him. But it messed him up good anyway."

"Phew, that was a close one," Lester said to himself.

But the ketchup just made the Furious Fry angrier. It regained its balance, wiped the ketchup out of its eyes with its gargantuan french-fry hands, and prepared once again to do some serious damage.

"What do we do now?" Lester yelled to Super Chicken Nugget Boy, who hurtled

back down to the ground on Arnie the Awesome
Amphibian's back.

"Don't worry!" said Super Chicken Nugget
Boy. "We got it covered."

The Furious Fry moved to squash Super Chicken Nugget Boy and Arnie just as they landed. But he was too late.

Boing!

Arnie the Awesome Amphibian's body was so slimy and rubbery that when he hit the ground, he and Super Chicken Nugget Boy bounced right off it.

"You are one sweet, springy salamander," said Super Chicken Nugget Boy as he and Arnie rose back into the air.

Squirt!

Super Chicken Nugget Boy unleashed another ketchup blast on the Furious Fry.

Splat!

"UUURRRGH!" The Furious Fry reached over to wipe the ketchup off him, but there was no point. Before he could even touch it . . .

Boing! Squirt! Splat!

Super Chicken Nugget Boy and Arnie bounced off the ground again and sent another ketchup cannon at the Furious Fry.

It kept going like that . . . until the Furious Fry was completely covered in layers and layers of ketchup, from head to toe. That was when Super Chicken Nugget Boy delivered the final blow.

"Take that, you forgettable fast-food flop!"

Splat!

He hit the Furious Fry with a supersonic squirt right in the gut. The Furious Fry looked down at its stomach and let out a pathetic little *"Uuurrrgh . . ."*

"What a fry-baby!" said Lester.

The Furious Fry flopped over and crashed into the ground, creating a giant pile of smashed potatoes.

16
GOOD FOOD GONE TO WASTE

$\mathbb{S}$uper Chicken Nugget Boy landed on top of Arnie the Awesome Amphibian and right next to Lester.

"That was amazing!" said Lester.

"I didn't do anything any other Super Chicken Nugget Boy with an Awesome Amphibian at his side wouldn't have done," said Super Chicken Nugget Boy.

"I guess you're right," said Lester. "But what made you think to use ketchup? I never would've thought to use it against a french fry. Ketchup is a french fry's best friend."

"That's true," said Chicken Nugget Boy,

"most of the time. But what's the one thing that ruins a perfectly good french fry?"

"I don't know," said Lester.

"Sogginess," said Super Chicken Nugget Boy. "Nothing's worse than a french fry that's been soaking in ketchup for too long. It loses all its crispiness, all its strength and power; it becomes a mushy, pathetic shell of its former self."

Shrieks of joy were heard in the distance as Super Chicken Nugget Boy's breading flaked off, and his body and Arnie's shrank back down to their normal sizes.

The kids from the school came running up to Fern, Lester, and Roy.

"Yay!"

"Whoo-hoo!"

"Ding-dong, the fry is dead!"

Ms. Durbindin followed behind the kids.

"Whew," she said. "For a minute there, I thought we were history. And not history in a good way, like the founding of America. History in a bad way, like getting squashed by the Furious Fry." She turned to Fern and Lester. "Did you boys see what happened?"

"We sure did!" said Lester. "It was Super Chicken Nugget Boy! He saved the day . . . with the help of one Awesome Amphibian!"

"So, where is this Super Chicken Nugget Boy?" asked Ms. Durbindin.

Lester looked at Fern.

"He's gone,"

said Fern, "to who knows where?"

"Well, that Nugget Chicken Super Boy is a true hero," said Principal Hamstone, walking up to the kids and Ms. Durbindin.

"He sure is," said Lester. "He's one brave chicken."

"Yeah, he's okay," said Fern. "But there's one thing he forgot to do."

"What's that?" asked Principal Hamstone.

"This!" said Fern.

He grabbed a piece of the fallen fry and flipped it up off the pile.

Everyone gasped.

There, beneath the rubble of the fry were Dirk and Snort sitting in front of a steering wheel and a control panel that said FURIOUS FRY STEERING WHEEL AND CONTROL PANEL.

"DIRRRRRRKWOOOOOD!" screamed Principal Hamstone.

"Uh . . ." said Dirk, "I can explain!"

"Don't you *I can explain, Daddy* me!" said
Principal Hamstone. "I've been waiting to say

this ever since you were in kindergarten, but your mother wouldn't let me. Well, now I'm going to say it, and I'm going to enjoy it. *Six months of detention!*"

"*Snort!*" said Snort in horror.

"You, too, Mr. Snortypants!" Principal Hamstone said.

Suddenly, another head popped out from under the fallen fry.

Everyone gasped again.

"You can't give my boy detention!" Mrs. Hamstone screamed.

"Oh, no?" said Principal Hamstone. "Not only am I giving him detention, I'm giving you detention too!"

"Are you crazy? I don't even go to this school."

"That's okay," said Principal Hamstone. "You can do it at home in the basement, from two fifty to four fifty every weekday. No TV! No computer! No phone!"

"But . . ." said Mrs. Hamstone.

"No buts!" said Principal Hamstone. "That's another six months for all of you."

Fern turned to Lester. "Let's get out of here," he said.

"Good idea," said Lester.

As they walked away from the school,

they could hear Dirk and Mrs. Hamstone still pleading their cases.

"You said you wouldn't help him, so we needed to take matters into our own hands," said Mrs. Hamstone.

"Besides," said Dirk, "we were just trying

to make the school safe from that stupid Chicken Nugget Boy."

"Let's make it a year and a half of detention!" said Principal Hamstone. "Woo! I love the sound of that!"

"I'm starving," said Fern to Lester. "You want to get something to eat?"

"You bet," said Lester. "Anything but french fries."

"You said it," said Fern. "Or chicken nuggets. Because that would be like eating myself, and I don't want to be a cannibal. That would be gross."

17

ONE LAST LITTLE NUGGET

You could say that things went back to normal at Bert Lahr Elementary School after Super Chicken Nugget Boy defeated the Furious Fry. But you'd be wrong.

The following day at school was like a celebration.

The second that school let out, the students ran out onto the playground, screaming and jumping for joy.

An entire day had gone by and not a single kid had been forced to obey any of Dirk's idiotic orders. No one had to pour shampoo into their shoes or put eggs in their ears or even eat any insects. It was a miracle!

Everyone was as happy as they'd ever been.

Everyone except for Dirk and Snort, that is. They were, of course, in detention.

"We'll see how tough that Stupid Chicken Numskull Boy is after he's attacked by a humongous hateful hamburger," said Dirk. "And maybe even a terrifying taco or two.

"Ha-ha-ha!" Dirk laughed as Snort snorted along.

"Put a lid on it!" screamed Mr. Pummel from the front of the room. "You don't want to make me come back there! You really, really don't!"

Meanwhile, out on the playground, kids played and partied as if they had just been freed from prison.

Principal Hamstone swung on the swings like a delighted little boy.

Fern and Lester played in the sandbox with Arnie Simpson the Salamander.

"What a relief to have that whole mess behind us," said Fern.

"Yeah," said Lester. "Finally, some peace and quiet."

"You can say that again," said Fern.

Lester was just about to say that again when suddenly, Allan Chen came running onto the playground!

"Run for your lives! Run for your lives!" he shouted. "Bowling Ball Barry just rolled into town, and he's knocking over everything he sees!"

"AAAAAAAGHHHHHHHH!!!"

Everybody screamed and ran for their lives.

Within seconds, the playground was empty. Only Fern, Lester, and Arnie remained.

"So much for peace and quiet," said Lester.

"You got that right," said Fern. "Bowling Ball Barry is the roughest, toughest bowling-ball bad guy around!"

"You ready?" asked Lester as he reached into his pocket and pulled out a packet of ketchup."

"Give it to us!" said Fern.

Splat! Splat!

Lester squirted Fern and Arnie with ketchup, and just like that . . .

Bam!

Super Chicken Nugget Boy and Arnie the Awesome Amphibian were back in business!

"We've got to stop this bowling-ball bozo before he strikes again!" said Super Chicken Nugget Boy. "Onward, Awesome Arnie! Onward!"

Super Chicken Nugget Boy jumped onto Arnie the Awesome Amphibian's back, and they zipped off the playground.

Zoom! Dirk and Snort watched as the crispy crime fighter sped past Mr. Pummel's windows.

"I can't stand that no-good nugget," Snort whispered under his breath.

"Don't worry," Dirk muttered back. "By the time we get through with him, he'll be nothing but a chicken salad."

"I can hear you!" screamed Mr. Pummel. "I don't like hearing you!"

Dirk and Snort slunk back into their seats as they watched Super Chicken Nugget

Boy ride off on Arnie the Awesome Amphibian to go do what he did best—defeat evil-doers, as only a Super Chicken Nugget Boy can do.